The Sweet Dreams EXPRESS

BEDTIME RIDE

ALL ABOARD!

Visit www.InnerCompassBooks.com to print or design your own ticket for *The Sweet Dreams Express*.

To my Dad, who has forever believed he is not a good sleeper;
yet whose bedtime words of wisdom inspired the creation of this book.

Note from the Author:

When I was a little girl, I had a hard time getting to sleep. Thanks to my busy mind, I spent hours bothering my parents, trying every technique under the sun and watching the numbers scroll by on the clock. Many years later, I eventually learned how to calm my mind for a restful sleep. *The Sweet Dreams Express* contains a culmination of techniques I use for myself and my children, along with words of wisdom from my dad, to help children learn positive sleep skills and become master sleepers. I wish every reader, young and old, the sweetest of dreams aboard *The Sweet Dreams Express*!

Acknowledgements:

Thank you to my team, my family, my tribe, and my readers for supporting me in the creation of Inner Compass Books. Aspen and Kendrix, thank you for being my creative sidekicks, for contributing ideas, and for being the reason I write. Matt, thank you for your support, for sharing your creativity, and for believing in me without a shadow of a doubt. Aleksandra, thank you for bringing this book to life with your artistic talent. Working with you was a delightful treat! Lacy, thank you for your editing expertise and wonderful guidance along the way.

The Sweet Dreams Express: A Meditative Bedtime Journey
Copyright © 2020 by Kristin Pierce

Written by Kristin Pierce
Illustrated by Aleksandra Szmidt
Edited by Lacy Lieffers of One Leaf Editing
Art direction, layout and cover design by Kristin Pierce
Artwork idea contributions by Aspen & Kendrix Pierce
Interior cover design by Matt Pierce

Inner Compass Books .com

Join our Insider's Club for free printable activities and more!
www.InnerCompassBooks.com

ISBN
978-1-99908-817-0 (Hardcover)
978-1-99908-816-3 (Paperback)

The Sweet Dreams
EXPRESS

by Kristin Pierce

Illustrated by Aleksandra Szmidt

It's getting late. It is that time.
Let's embark on a bedtime rhyme.

For as you sleep,
    your body works

To heal and grow
    and mend the quirks;

Unwinds your mind
to free the day,

And helps emotions
float away.

Hello my friend. Please be my guest
To journey on this bedtime quest.

The **Sweet Dreams EXPRESS**

ENTER

RULES:

Prior to boarding,
please:

1. Put on pajamas.

2. Brush your teeth.

3. Use the bathroom.

4. Climb into bed.

5. Get your ticket.

Follow the cues—tried, tested, and true—
To help you sleep the whole night through.

Are you ready? Come on, let's see.
You'll master this. Just follow me.

TICKETS

Free your wiggles;
    move hands and feet.
Stretch arms and legs
    to your own beat.

Reach way up high,
    then touch your toes.

Stretch side to side;
    move nice and slow.

Touch chin to chest,
    then hug your knees.
Pull them in close,
    now gently squeeze.

ALL ABOARD The Sweet Dreams Express!

Please choose a cozy spot to rest.

Fluff your pillow,
and rest your head.

Feel your body
sink down in bed.

Begin with breath;
in nice and slow.
Exhale slowly,
and find your flow.

Melt your worries;
blow out your stress.
Relax your mind.
It's time to rest.

INHALE

EXHALE

Just fill your lungs, and then release

To find within a place of peace.

SQUEEZE your muscles, and then relax,
Let your body feel loose and lax.

SQUEEZE

RELAX

HUG yourself TIGHT
and count one, two.

Then feel the calm wash right through you.

HUG...1...2...

Now, close your eyes and move inside.
Breathe in real deep. It's time to find
Just where your mind feels stuck and bound
With thoughts and feelings tightly wound.

Scan your body
    from head to toe.
Find heavy spots
    that block your flow.

Breathe through each
    blockage with your air;
With gentle hands
    show it you care.

Then watch it shift
    and feel it swirl.
Blow it all out;
    let it untwirl.

Each heavy spot
that tries to stay;
Grab it, pull it,
toss it away.

Repeat until
the "stuck" is gone.

Release it with
a great big yawn.

Next up, some special sleepy dust...

Its twinkly magic is a must.

Move your fingers.
Hear it sprinkle.
Feel it land and
make you tingle.

A mind massage does soothe and sway
Allow your thoughts to drain away.

Touch the space between your brow
To power down your mind right now.

Go on and rest your weary head. Relax and melt down into bed.

Now, feel the night wrap you up tight.
And focus on one shining light.

Follow it to where dreams are made.

Allow that twinkling star to fade.

You're almost there;
all tucked in tight.

Just snuggle up,
and say, "Goodnight."

Now, float into the deepest sleep.

The sweetest dreams are yours to keep.

And in the night if you do wake,
Just start again for goodness sake!

You can do it. You know it's true.
A master sleeper—yes, that's you.

Free your wiggles;
climb into bed.

Then find your breath;
unload your head.

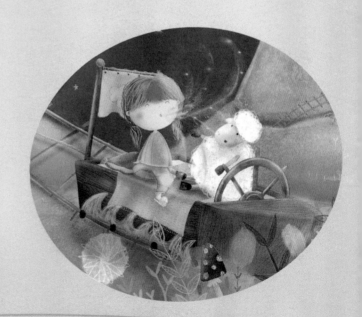

Release your stuck,
and calm your mind.

Use sleepy dust;
    then you must find

The special space
    between your brow,
        To power down
            your mind right now.

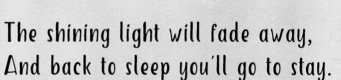

The shining light will fade away,
And back to sleep you'll go to stay.

When you awake
so fresh and bright,

You'll glow just like
the new sunlight.

Ready to start
the day anew.

And feeling like
a brand new you.

About the Author

Photo by Nancy Newby Photography

Kristin Pierce is an award-winning author, a self-awareness educator, and the founder of Inner Compass Books. It is her mission to create mindfully-crafted children's books that encourage kids to question their limits, pursue their passions, utilize the power of their minds, and dream bigger than belief.

The Sweet Dreams Express is her fourth children's book.

She lives in Saskatchewan, Canada with her husband, two children, and their dog.

Other Titles from Inner Compass Books:

To learn more, visit **www.InnerCompassBooks.com**
or find Kristin on Facebook and Instagram @InnerCompassBooks

Made in the USA
Las Vegas, NV
18 April 2021